Daniel Gets Scared

adapted by Maggie Testa
based on the screenplay "A Stormy Day"
written by Wendy Harris
poses and layouts by Jason Fruchter

Ready-to-Read

Simon Spotlight
New York   London   Toronto   Sydney   New Delhi

SIMON SPOTLIGHT
An imprint of Simon & Schuster Children's Publishing Division
1230 Avenue of the Americas, New York, New York 10020
This Simon Spotlight edition September 2020
© 2015 The Fred Rogers Company. All rights reserved.
All rights reserved, including the right of reproduction in whole or in part in any form.
SIMON SPOTLIGHT, READY-TO-READ, and colophon are registered trademarks of Simon & Schuster, Inc.
For information about special discounts for bulk purchases, please contact Simon & Schuster Special Sales at
1-866-506-1949 or business@simonandschuster.com.
Manufactured in the United States of America 0621 LAK
4 6 8 10 9 7 5 3
ISBN 978-1-4814-5259-5 (eBook)
ISBN 978-1-5344-7336-2 (prop)

O the Owl is here to play.

"Time to go inside," calls Mom.

"It got dark, and then we heard a boom. We got scared," I say.

"There is something I do when I am scared," says Mom.

"When you are scared," says Mom, "close your eyes and think of something happy."

Books make him happy.
He feels a little
less scared now.

Boom!

We hear more thunder.

It scares us again.

"When you are scared, close your eyes and think of something happy," I said.

When you are scared,
close your eyes and
think of something happy!
Ugga Mugga!